Tami Lehman-Wilzig

SOOSiE
THE HORSE
THAT SAVED SHABBAT

ILLUSTRATED BY
Menahem Halberstadt

Kalaniot Books
Moosic, Pennsylvania

LONG AGO, Jerusalem was a tiny town of narrow cobblestone streets and low stone houses. A bakery stood in the middle of the town. It had two large, open windows, letting the aroma of freshly baked goods waft in and out of the surrounding homes.

Every Friday morning when the sky was still dark and the stars still bright, the bakery's elderly owners, Esther and Ezra, got out of bed and slowly walked to the bakery. Ezra lit the large oven, then they mixed and kneaded the dough. When the dough was ready, they braided one challah after another. After lining up the loaves on a large baking pan, Ezra slid them into the oven.

By the time the sun came up, the couple had baked enough
challah for all the families in Jerusalem to bless and eat at their
Shabbat dinners.

Jacob, their delivery boy, always arrived soon after. He filled the wagon with challah. Next, he led Esther and Ezra's beloved horse Soosie out of her stall. He gave her a big hug, whispered in her ear, and hitched her to the wagon.

Climbing into the driver's seat, Jacob clicked his tongue three times. Soosie nodded her head up and down, neighing back three times. Then she swished her tail, and the two were on their way.

CLIP-CLOP, CLIP-CLOP. Soosie's hooves echoed on the cobblestones of Jerusalem Road. With another click of his tongue, Jacob signaled Soosie to stop so the families could buy their loaves of challah.

"Yummm," the people murmured, holding the loaves close to their hearts. "Our day of rest would not be complete without Esther and Ezra's challah."

CLINK-CLANG, CLINK-CLANG. Coins dropped
into a tin bank as each family paid.

"Shabbat Shalom!" everyone called out as they went back
to their houses. Jacob clicked his tongue three times. Soosie
nodded her head up and down, neighing back three times.
She swished her tail and headed for the next stop.

CLIP-CLOP, CLIP-CLOP. Jacob guided Soosie onto Zion Street. The wagon came to a stop.

CLINK-CLANG, CLINK-CLANG went the coins as
they were dropped into the tin bank.

"Shabbat Shalom!" the people called out as Jacob clicked
his tongue three times. Soosie neighed back three times,
swished her tail, and headed for the next stop.

CLIP...CLOP...CLIP...CLOP. Soosie walked slowly up the steep hill on Hillel Street. People watched and clapped when the wagon reached the top.

CLINK-CLANG, CLINK-CLANG went the coins as they were dropped into the tin bank.

"Shabbat Shalom!" the people called out, watching Jacob feed a tired Soosie some apple slices. Soosie munched while Jacob jumped up into the driver's seat. He clicked his tongue three times. Soosie neighed back three times, swished her tail, and headed for the next stop.

Their delivery route continued with a left turn, a right turn, a **CLIP** and a **CLOP,** a **CLINK** and a **CLANG,** till the entire town had challah for Shabbat.

And so it went week after week, month after month, until . . .

One Friday morning, Jacob came to the bakery looking sick. "You should be in bed!" exclaimed Esther.

"After the deliveries," answered Jacob, sitting down, holding his head.

"Esther is right. You aren't well," said Ezra, bringing Jacob a glass of water.

Slowly sipping, Jacob replied, "I'll do . . . the deliveries. I
know . . . you can't. I know that you are tired and achy."
"You can barely talk!" replied Ezra, swaying and praying
for a solution as their large clock tick-tocked the time away.

Meanwhile, the scent of Shabbat challah filled the bakery. It floated out the windows to Soosie's stall. Soosie's nostrils fluttered. The smell grew stronger, so she snorted. Finally, she neighed and stomped her hoofs. After all, it was Friday morning!

When Jacob heard Soosie, his pale face suddenly
lit up. "Soosie knows the way!" he announced.
"Soosie can deliver the challah by herself!"
"Soosie?" asked a bewildered Esther and Ezra.
"Yes, she can do it!" insisted Jacob.

With great hesitation, they loaded the wagon. Esther sighed and Ezra shrugged as he put the tin bank on the driver's seat and placed a large note underneath it. "Jacob is sick today. Please take your challah loaves and drop your money into the bank. Shabbat Shalom!"

Ezra hitched Soosie to the wagon. Jacob whispered into Soosie's ear. She nodded her head. Jacob clicked his tongue three times. Soosie answered with three neighs. Then she swished her tail and went on her way.

CLIP-CLOP, CLIP-CLOP went Soosie's hooves.
The people at the first stop fidgeted. "You're late," they
started to say but stopped when they realized Soosie was
on her own. They read the note and passed it around.

CLINK-CLANG, CLINK-CLANG went the coins as they dropped into the tin bank. Once the people called out, "Shabbat Shalom!" Soosie neighed, swished her tail, and headed for the next stop.

Back at the bakery, Esther and Ezra anxiously waited
for Soosie to return, while Jacob slept near her stall.
When two hours passed they cupped their ears, hoping
to hear the sound of Soosie's hooves.

"Maybe Soosie forgot the route!"
said Esther. "Maybe she hurt a leg!
Maybe the wagon broke down!"

Three hours passed.

Esther and Ezra strained their necks,
looking up and down the street

. . . but no Soosie.

FINALLY . . . they heard
CLIP...CLOP...CLIP...CLOP...CLIP...CLOP.

A tired Soosie entered the bakery's backyard, swished her tail, yawned, and bowed her head. The wagon was empty. The tin bank was full.

Esther stroked Soosie's mane. Ezra released Soosie from the
harness, brought her a bowl of water and a scoop of grain.
Soosie whinnied, then clip-clopped to her stall, softly licking
Jacob's ear on her way. He opened his eyes and smiled.

"You've earned your day of rest," Ezra whispered.
With a snoozy snort, Soosie closed her eyes.
"Shabbat Shalom!" said Esther softly as she and
Ezra tiptoed back to the bakery.

SOME NOTES FROM THE AUTHOR

This tale was inspired by the history of Angel Bakery—one of Israel's largest bakery chains. Its first bakery was established by Salomon Angel in 1927, in the Jerusalem neighborhood of Bayit VeGan. Salomon was inspired by his father, who imported flour in order to bake and sell bread in the store he owned, located in Jerusalem's Old City. Years later in a newspaper interview, Salomon's son Danny recalled how one time his grandfather's delivery boy was sick, so he relied on the horse who pulled the bread cart to deliver bread to his customers. That brief recollection motivated me to create a folktale about challah in Jerusalem.

What Is Shabbat?

Shabbat—the Sabbath day, also known as *Shabbos*—is a weekly day of rest, and its origins go back to the Ten Commandments. The Fourth Commandment states: "Honor the Sabbath." In the Bible, Exodus 31:16–17 explains: "The Israelites are to observe the Sabbath, celebrating it for the generations to come as a lasting covenant. It will be a sign between Me and the Israelites forever, for in six days God made the heavens and the earth, and on the seventh day God rested and was refreshed."

Celebrating Shabbat

Shabbat begins a few minutes before the sun sets on Friday evening. It ends when three stars can be seen in the sky on Saturday night. Jews celebrate with blessings over candles, wine, and special braided bread called challah. Many Jews say a blessing over two loaves of challah on Shabbat. The two loaves are symbolic of the double portion of food called manna, an edible substance that fell from heaven on Fridays when the Children of Israel were in the wilderness for forty years after leaving Egypt. With a double portion of manna, they had enough food to get them through the entire Shabbat.

Shabbat Blessings

BLESSING OVER THE CANDLES: Blessed are You, God, Ruler of the universe, who sanctified us with the commandment of lighting Shabbat candles.

Baruch atah Adonai, Eloheinu Melech haolam, asher kid'shanu b'mitzvotav vitzivanu l'hadlik ner shel Shabbat.

בָּרוּךְ אַתָּה ה׳ אֱלֹהֵינוּ מֶלֶךְ הָעוֹלָם אֲשֶׁר קִדְּשָׁנוּ בְּמִצְוֹתָיו וְצִוָּנוּ לְהַדְלִיק נֵר שֶׁל שַׁבָּת.

BLESSING OVER THE WINE: Blessed are You, God, Ruler of the universe, Creator of the fruit of the vine.

Baruch atah Adonai, Eloheinu Melech haolam, borei p'ri hagafen.

בָּרוּךְ אַתָּה ה׳ אֱלֹהֵינוּ מֶלֶךְ הָעוֹלָם בּוֹרֵא פְּרִי הַגָּפֶן.

BLESSING OVER THE CHALLAH: Blessed are You, God, Ruler of the universe, who has brought forth bread from the earth.

Baruch atah Adonai, Eloheinu Melech haolam, hamotzi lechem min ha'aretz.

בָּרוּךְ אַתָּה ה׳ אֱלֹהֵינוּ מֶלֶךְ הָעוֹלָם הַמּוֹצִיא לֶחֶם מִן הָאָרֶץ.

Animal Rights Is Part of Shabbat

Ezra and Esther follow the Bible's teachings about protecting animals. The Bible tells us Shabbat is a time of rest for everyone—even animals. Just like people, all animals that have worked hard during the week should have a day to rest.

About the Name Soosie

The word for horse in Hebrew is *soos*: סוס. Soosie is a name of endearment meaning "my horse."

About the People of Jerusalem

Jerusalem has always been one big melting pot. The people you meet in this book illustrate that. Since ancient times and through the period known as the Diaspora, when many were forced to leave Israel, Jerusalem has been a holy city for Jews. After the Crusades, Jews from the Middle East and North Africa, also known as Sephardim, began to return to their homeland. With the Spanish Expulsion in 1492, many more Sephardim traveled east to the Land of Israel, which was then controlled by the Ottomans. The first Bukharan Jews arrived from central Asia in the 1870s and established Jerusalem's Bukharan Quarter. In the 1880s Yemenite Jews began settling in Jerusalem, as did Ashkenazi Jews from Eastern Europe. Today in Jerusalem you can find Jews from all over the world. And while they might look very different from each other, they all share a love for this holy city.

For my father of blessed memory,
Dr. Emil Lehman, whose deep love of the Jewish heritage has had a lasting impact on me.
—T. L.-W.

For my beloved family, and our delicious Shabbat challahs. **—M. H.**